Glitterwings Academy

Book Three

Friends Forever

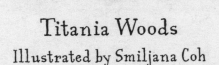

Titania Woods

Illustrated by Smiljana Coh

BLOOMSBURY

LONDON BERLIN NEW YORK

To Christopher

Bloomsbury Publishing, London, Berlin and New York

First published in Great Britain in 2008 by Bloomsbury Publishing Plc
36 Soho Square, London, W1D 3QY

This edition published in 2009

A CIP catalogue record of this book is available from the British Library

ISBN 978 1 4088 0488 9

FSC
Mixed Sources
Product group from well-managed
forests and other controlled sources
Cert no. SGS - COC - 2061
www.fsc.org
© 1996 Forest Stewardship Council

Typeset by Dorchester Typesetting Group Ltd
Printed in Great Britain by Clays Ltd, St Ives Plc

1 3 5 7 9 10 8 6 4 2

www.glitterwingsacademy.co.uk

Chapter One

'Now then, class.' Madame Brightfoot hovered in front of the Daffodil Branch fairies and patted her bright purple hair into place. 'Today we learn a new dance! Today, we learn how to find creatures in distress.'

Twink Flutterby shot an excited glance at Bimi, her best friend. 'Glimmery!' she whispered. It was a fairy's duty to take care of nature, but as first-year students, Twink and her friends hadn't had many chances to do this yet.

Bimi's dark blue eyes shone. 'I wonder if we'll

actually get to help something?'

A thrill rippled through Twink's wings. 'Oh, I hope so! I'd love to tell my parents that.' Twink's parents were both Fairy Medics, and it was Twink's dearest wish to follow in their wing strokes some day.

'Form a circle!' called Madame, waving her slender arms. 'Quick, quick!'

Madame Brightfoot's Dance class was held in an enchanted ring of mushrooms near the wood. Behind them, the great oak tree that housed Glitterwings Academy was ablaze with autumn, its leaves on fire with red and gold and orange. Hundreds of tiny windows wound their way up the tree's trunk, and the grand double doors at its base looked shiny and welcoming.

The Daffodil Branch fairies stood in a circle, holding hands.

'Flower position!' Madame shot up into the air, her spiderweb dress shimmering.

The fairies opened their wings so that the very tips of them touched. Twink squeezed Bimi's hand.

Across the circle, she saw her friend Sooze bouncing on her toes, and she grinned. Sooze loved trying anything new!

Clasping her hands, Madame slowly sank back down to earth. Her voice was low and solemn. 'Now, this dance is very different from the others you've learned. It is a most serious dance.'

She looked around the circle, her expression grave. Twink swallowed. The class grew very still as they all gazed back at her.

Finally Madame nodded. 'Close your eyes, everyone.'

Twink shut her eyes, listening closely as Madame went on.

'You must all concentrate together on hearing any nearby creatures in distress – and with the magic of the dance, you'll be able to understand what they're telling you if they respond. Now . . . two skips left, two skips right, dip, twirl, and rise.'

They began to dance. The air felt alive with sparkles as the magic gathered.

'Now rise!' said Madame's voice.

The fairies lifted into the air, their wings humming softly. 'Again!' directed Madame. 'Concentrate!'

Does anything need our help? thought Twink as her feet moved in the air.

They repeated the dance over and over. The magic swelled until it felt like a thousand tiny bubbles swirling around them – and still the dance went on. Wasn't anything going to happen?

Are there any creatures that need our help? thought Twink again, concentrating harder than ever. *We want to help you!*

Suddenly she heard it: a small, frightened voice inside her head. *Yes!* it called. *Help me, please!* Twink gasped, and almost dropped Bimi's hand.

Where are you? she thought eagerly.

The little voice came again. *In the wood! Please help me!*

We will! thought Twink as loudly as she could. *Don't worry, we're coming!*

'Stop the dance!' shouted Madame suddenly. 'All land!'

Twink's eyes flew open. She and Bimi stared at each other as they drifted down to the ground.

'Did you hear it, too?' whispered Twink.

Bimi nodded, her eyes wide. 'It sounded so scared! What was it?'

'You might well ask!' said Madame, overhearing her. She shook her purple head. 'Ah, this is a most unfortunate thing. But it is a lesson you all must learn sometime. Who can tell me what that voice was?'

The class stared blankly at her. In the silence, a large bumblebee bobbed past. Finally Pix raised her hand. 'Was it a sort of bird?'

'No, not a bird!' said Madame. The fairies looked at each other in surprise. Pix always got the right answer.

'It was something dreadful, something awful!' A shiver ran through Madame's silver wings. 'Dear children . . . that voice you heard was a *wasp*.'

A wasp! A startled gasp ran through the class. Twink felt like icy water had been thrown over her. The Great Wasp Wars had ended centuries ago,

The Wood

the fairies had never forgotten the terrible things the wasps had done.

Madame nodded grimly. 'Yes, a wasp. Now you know what they sound like. Never forget! It is a voice to shun!'

Twink bit her lip as she thought of the tiny voice, pl... help. Maybe it had been a wasp, but it ... alone – so frightened. She slowly

... e smoothed her hair.

... help it?' asked Twink.

Madame's eyes bulged. She opened her mouth and shut it again.

Twink gulped. 'I mean – well, I know it's a wasp and everything, but it's hurt. It's out there in the wood somewhere, and –'

'Enough!' cried Madame, flinging her hands dramatically over her ears. 'We do not help wasps! No fairy has helped a wasp for a thousand years – they are treacherous, vile creatures.'

Twink's wings felt clammy. Everyone was staring at her, wide-eyed with horror. Even Sooze looked alarmed. 'I – I just thought – we're supposed to help nature –' she stammered.

'Not *that* sort of nature,' snapped Madame. 'Not another word, Twink! Now, everyone join hands and we'll do the happy breeze dance, to blow these unpleasant thoughts away.'

They did the happy breeze dance, but it didn't cheer Twink up much – not even when the merry wind tickled her wings and toes. As they flew back to school after class, she glanced over her shoulder at the wood, wondering where the wasp was. Was it badly hurt?

Bimi jostled her with a wing. 'Twink, you're not still thinking about that wasp, are you?'

Twink hesitated. 'It's hurt, that's all.'

'Oh, Twink!' Bimi made a face. 'It was probably only *pretending* to be hurt, to trick us! You can't trust wasps – everyone knows that.'

'Maybe,' said Twink doubtfully.

They flew into the school with the rest of Daffodil Branch. Inside, Glitterwings was a high tower of golden light, with fairies darting in and out of its many branches.

'Fairy Dust class next!' cried Bimi. 'Come on!'

Their wings blurred as they jetted upwards. Their Fairy Dust lessons were held near the very top of the tree – it was always a race to get there on time after Dance class!

Twink banked left to avoid a chattering crowd of hovering Third Years. 'But, Bimi, listen!' she panted. 'What if it wasn't pretending? What if it really needed help?'

Bimi shook her head. 'Then let another wasp help

it! Honestly, Twink, what's wrong with you? Think about the Great Wasp Wars!'

Twink sighed. 'I suppose you're right.'

'I *know* I am!' laughed Bimi in exasperation.

With a quick hop, they landed on the ledge of their Fairy Dust classroom. Smoothing her wind-messed pink hair, Twink flitted to one of the spotted mushroom seats.

Bimi sat beside her, and the two girls smiled at each other. They had been best friends since their first term at Glitterwings, and Twink knew that no one was more sensible or fair-minded than Bimi.

She's right, Twink decided. *I'll forget about the wasp.*

Bimi was also one of the prettiest fairies in the school, with her midnight-blue hair and gold and silver wings. Twink often felt very plain beside her. Her own wings were just boring old lavender!

'Well, *that* was a glimmery Dance lesson, wasn't it?' Sooze swooped into the room and landed with a bounce. 'Talking to a wasp – ugh!'

She gave an exaggerated shudder, and several of

the girls laughed. The young fairies all lived in Daffodil Branch together, and all wore yellow or white daffodil dresses, along with the school's jaunty oak-leaf caps.

Miss Sparkle arrived, and the class took their seats. 'Good morning,' she said in her dry voice. 'Today we are going to discuss how to use fairy dust in the dark.'

Twink held back a groan as she pulled out her pink petal-pad to take notes. She could hardly wait to be a second-year student, when they could actually *use* fairy dust, instead of just talking about it!

'Now then.' Miss Sparkle folded her thin white wings behind her back and regarded them sternly. 'Although fairy dust glows in the dark, this is only a reflection of the moonlight. Therefore, on moonless nights, you must . . .'

Twink's snail-trail pen slowed as she thought of the wasp, pleading for help.

No, she thought firmly. *Bimi's right. It was just a trick.* And taking a deep breath, she started to write again.

The Great Branch was the largest branch in the school – a long, wide space lined with mossy green tables and spotted mushroom seats. A different flower hung over each table for each of the dorms, so that the Branch was like a springtime garden, bursting with colour. Glow-worm lanterns hung from the ceiling, and arched windows let in the sunlight.

Dinner that night was a crunchy autumn nut cake, served with a sweet nectar sauce. The fairies murmured in appreciation as the school's butterflies flowed into the Great Branch, lightly dropping an oak-leaf platter on to each table.

Twink loved nut cake, but somehow she didn't feel very hungry. She glanced at the windows. Twilight was coming. Was it very dark in the wood, she wondered?

'What's up, Opposite?' asked Sooze from across the table.

Twink forced a smile. 'Nothing,' she said.

Sooze had bright lavender hair and pink wings, and Twink had the opposite, hence Sooze's

12

nickname for her. The two girls had been best friends once, and were still close – even though Twink knew that Sooze wasn't always very dependable!

'Still mooning about that wasp, I suppose!' sneered a pointed-faced fairy from the end of the table.

Mariella! Twink bit back her response.

'Watch it, you,' said Sooze sharply. 'Remember what happened last term!'

The term before, the entire first year had stopped talking to Mariella when Twink and her friends had caught her out in a nasty prank she'd played against Bimi. Mariella's cheeks reddened at the mention of it. Clapping her pale green wings shut, she scowled down at her acorn cup.

Her friend Lola, sitting beside her, squeaked, 'But Mariella didn't do anything – it was Twink! Imagine wanting to help a wasp! That's something only a real wasp brain would do.'

Lola laughed loudly at her own joke. Mariella snickered, and flipped back her silvery-green hair.

The rest of the table fell silent. Twink's face burned. Even though nobody liked Mariella or Lola, Twink could tell that her friends agreed with them.

'Oh, come on – she just felt sorry for it, that's all,' put in Bimi. 'I did too, until I knew what it was.'

Pix fluttered her yellow wings doubtfully. 'Yes, but still . . .'

'You can never trust a wasp!' put in Sili, an excitable fairy with silver hair. Her large eyes widened, and she lowered her voice. 'Why, my father said that –'

'Will everyone just stop!' burst out Twink. 'I *haven't* helped a wasp, and I'm not going to!'

'Well . . . that's all right, then,' said Sooze with a sudden grin.

Everyone laughed, and Twink felt herself relax. Suddenly she was starving. She picked up her nut cake and took a bite. Of course she wasn't going to help a wasp! The whole thing was just silly.

After dinner, Miss Shimmery, the HeadFairy of Glitterwings Academy, hovered above the platform at the front of the Great Branch. 'Your attention, please!' she called, clapping her hands. Her rainbow wings gleamed like opals in the light of the glow-worm lanterns.

The school turned towards her, their faces expectant. Miss Shimmery smiled. 'I've an announcement to make,' she said in her strong, low voice. 'We're going to have a special project this term, and we'd like the whole school to participate.'

A buzz of interest rippled through the Branch. Miss Shimmery held up her hands for silence. Her

Miss Shimmery

white hair looked like a piece of cloud.

'We'd like for each and every student to do something for the betterment of the school,' she went on. 'You can write a song, or make something, or create a new spell – anything you like! But whatever you choose should improve our beloved school in some way.'

Her eyes held a faint twinkle as she scanned the crowd. 'You have two weeks,' she added. 'At the end of that time we'll have a contest, and the best three projects from each year will win sparkle marks for their branches!'

Miss Shimmery drifted back down to the platform. The Great Branch erupted in eager conversation.

Sooze bounced on her seat, fluttering her wings. 'Glimmery! I'm going to invent a new dance. Madame will love it!'

Pix looked thoughtful. 'I think I'll write about the history of Glitterwings,' she said. 'I bet there's loads of fascinating stuff in the library! What about you, Twink?'

Twink shook her head. 'I'm not sure yet.' As the conversation went on, she saw that Bimi had a worried expression on her face. 'What's wrong?' she whispered.

Bimi sighed. 'Oh, I'm no good at this sort of thing! Everyone else's project is sure to be better than mine. You're all so clever.'

Twink started to laugh, and then stopped. Bimi was serious. 'But we're not!' she protested. 'Only Pix is really brainy; the rest of us are just ordinary. You're as clever as any of us.'

But she could tell that Bimi wasn't convinced. She rubbed her lavender wing against Bimi's gold and silver one. 'Why don't I help you?' she suggested. 'I mean, if you're really worried about it.'

Relief burst across Bimi's face. '*Would* you? Twink, that would be glimmery!'

'Of course I will,' said Twink. 'Don't worry, we'll do it together!'

As the fairies got ready for bed that night, Twink lingered by the Daffodil Branch window. Under the moonlit sky, she could just see the dark outline of the wood. Was the wasp still out there, somewhere? Twink shook herself impatiently. Why was she even still thinking of it?

'Glow-worms out in two minutes!' called Mrs Hover, the matron. Her stout footsteps echoed as she bustled about the branch. 'Twink! You're not even dressed for bed yet, you silly fairy! Come on, flitter-flutter.'

'Sorry, Mrs Hover!' Hastily, Twink pulled on her soft cobweb nightgown and hopped into bed. The cheerful yellow daffodil that hung overhead swayed slightly.

'Goodnight, Twink,' said Bimi sleepily from the next bed. Her long hair spilled across her cotton-bud pillow like a field of bluebells.

Twink pulled her petal duvet up under her chin. 'Goodnight, Bimi.'

'Glow-worms out,' ordered Mrs Hover. 'Goodnight, my dears!' Daffodil Branch fell into darkness as Mrs Hover left, closing the door behind her.

Twink turned in her bed, trying to get comfortable. What was wrong with her, anyway? Everything was just as it should be. Her moss bed was welcoming and cosy. Her best friend was right beside her, and on her bedside mushroom, the drawings of her family smiled at her in the moonlight.

Why did she feel so troubled?

Chapter
Two

The wasp huddled under a fallen log, shivering in the chill autumn night. Though he longed to fly home to his family, he couldn't. One of his wings lay bent and crumpled against his striped back.

The wasp was very young – only a baby, really – and now he blinked back tears. The night was so dark, and he was alone. What had happened to the friendly voices that had found him that morning? One of them had seemed especially kind, and had said they'd come and help him.

But no one had come.

An owl called somewhere in the wood, and the wasp trembled. What in waspdom was he going to do? His parents didn't know where he was. Nobody did.

Then it came to him. The voices had found *him*, so perhaps he could find the voices, if he tried! Closing his eyes, the wasp concentrated as hard as he could. *Help me! Please! I'm here in the wood! I need help!*

Nothing happened. The wasp refused to give up. He thought even harder, calling out to the friendly voice that had promised to help him.

The moon moved slowly across the sky as the night passed.

Help me! Please!

Twink awoke with a start. The wasp! It was calling for her, pleading for help. But no, it *couldn't* have called to her – wasps didn't have magic. It was just a dream, that was all.

Twink frowned uncertainly. It had seemed so real . . .

21

Stop it! she told herself. *It was only a dream. You really are a wasp brain if you get so upset over it!* Pulling her covers up over her ears, Twink closed her eyes and tried to go back to sleep.

Can't you hear me? Please help! I'm in the wood!

Twink gasped as her eyes flew open again. She hadn't imagined it. The voice was really calling to her.

Heart pounding, she sat up and looked out of the window. There were still stars in the lightening sky. No one would be up for a while yet. She had time to go and find the wasp, if she hurried!

Twink started to push back her covers. Then she saw Bimi's sleeping figure, and hesitated. Bimi wouldn't understand. Nobody would.

Help . . .

The voice came again, fainter this time. Twink made up her mind. Taking care not to wake the others, she hastily pulled on her clothes and pushed her pillow under her covers, in case Mrs Hover glanced in.

Easing the door open, Twink slipped out of

Daffodil Branch. A moment later, she was spiralling down the dark trunk of the school, passing silent branches full of sleeping fairies.

Midway down, Twink paused, hovering in place. How was she going to get out? The great front doors would be locked now! Suddenly she remembered – there was a broken window latch in their Flower Power classroom. Miss Petal had complained about it just the other day.

Twink plunged down into the darkness, turning sharply to dive into a branch corridor. The Flower Power branch was halfway down, jutting off on its own. *Oh, please don't let the door be locked!* Landing on the ledge, she wiped her hands on her daffodil skirt and tried it.

The door slipped open easily. Twink let out a breath and sped into the moonlit room, half-flying and half-running.

Which window was it? Twink glanced at the row that marched down the branch. There, that one! A moment later she was tugging gently at its wooden latch. It hadn't been fixed yet, and the window

swung open. Cool night air swirled into the room.

Twink gulped. Should she really do this? Leaving the school at night was a serious matter – she and her friends had got into awful trouble for it last term. Then she thought of the voice again, and knew she didn't have a choice. She flitted up and squeezed through the narrow frame.

Suddenly Twink was hovering outside, halfway up the school. The wood crouched darkly across the fields.

'All right,' she murmured. 'I don't know where you are, or how I can help you – but I'm going to try!'

Taking a deep breath, she flew towards the wood as fast as she could.

The wood seemed to grow darker and more forbidding the nearer she got to it. Twink stopped on its edge, biting her lip. How was she ever going to find one wasp in a wood this size?

Help! Help me!

Twink turned in the air, listening hard. Yes, he

was that way! She dived into the wood, flying fast, darting around trees and undergrowth.

The voice led her to the very deepest, darkest heart of the wood. Suddenly Twink remembered what Bimi had said, and her wings felt cold. Had the wasp lured her to this remote spot for some treacherous reason?

Help me!

Twink spun about, peering at the trees and bushes around her. It was coming from under that fallen log! She swallowed, staring at the dark space. Did she dare? What if her friends were right?

Then she heard it: a tiny sobbing sound. Twink's eyes widened. The wasp was crying!

Sympathy rushed through her. She swooped towards the fallen log, landing neatly in front of it. 'Hello, are you there?' she called. 'Please stop crying! I've come to help you!'

There was a soft snuffling noise, and a rustling. Suddenly Twink saw it crawling towards her in the moonlight: a little baby wasp with a broken wing.

'Oh!' gasped Twink. She knelt beside the wasp.

'You poor thing!'

The wasp nuzzled at her hand, humming slightly. Twink could feel his relief as clearly as if it were her own. And in that moment, she knew she had lost her heart completely. The wasp was her responsibility now, and she would never let it down.

'But what am I going to do with you?' she whispered, stroking his head. 'I can't just leave you here!' She glanced at the sky. It was lighter now. She had to get back to school before everyone woke up!

'I'll hide you somewhere close to school,' she told

the wasp. 'I think I know just the place. Then I'll see what I can do about healing your wing.'

How could she heal him on her own, though? She was only a First Year! Pushing aside her doubts, Twink wrapped her arms around the wasp and picked him up.

He gave a buzz and clung to her with his spindly legs, flapping his good wing in alarm. 'Shush!' Twink told him. 'It's OK. I just have to get you back to school.'

The wasp quietened, and Twink took off, skimming quickly back the way she had come. When she reached Glitterwings, she saw with relief that the school's windows were still dark.

Shifting the wasp in her arms, Twink flitted around to the back of the school. There was a small dell here, with an abandoned tree stump that she and Bimi had found one day. It used to be a care-taker's cottage, but no one had lived there for years.

The tree stump was half-hidden by long grasses. Pushing her way through them, Twink flew through the doorway.

Inside it was dark and run-down, but dry, and cosy enough. With a sigh of relief, Twink placed the wasp on the mossy bed in the corner. 'There!' she said. 'You'll be all right here, won't you?'

The wasp curled up contentedly, humming to himself. Looking around, Twink saw an old walnut-bucket. 'I'll be right back!' she told the wasp.

She grabbed the bucket and flew hastily down to the pond. Filling it with water, she returned to the stump and placed it beside the wasp. He drank gratefully for a long time, flapping his good wing, and then curled up again with a satisfied buzz.

'Right,' said Twink. 'Let's look at your wing!'

She inspected it carefully in the faint light, and her spirits sank. It was badly broken. The wasp watched her anxiously as she gently poked and prodded.

'Oh, I'm sure I can fix that!' said Twink, trying to hide how worried she felt. 'I just need to – to do a bit of research, that's all.'

The wasp seemed relieved. Humming, he climbed into Twink's lap. The faint dawn streamed through a

Stripe

hole in the ceiling, showing his yellow and black stripes.

Twink stroked his soft back. 'You need a name, don't you?' she said. 'Or do you have one already?'

The wasp stopped humming and looked blankly at her. Twink grinned. 'All right, let me think . . . I know! I'll call you Stripe.'

Stripe seemed to approve of his new name. He buzzed loudly, tickling Twink's face with his good wing. She laughed. 'Stripe it is, then!'

Suddenly Twink realised that it wasn't as dark

inside the stump as it had been. Oh, wasps, it was almost daylight!

She leapt up. 'I've got to go – I'll be back later with some food!'

The wasp looked at her with a worried expression. 'It's all right, I'll be back,' said Twink. 'But I've got to go now.'

Had he understood? She couldn't tell. With a final hasty stroke of his back, Twink flew from the stump. Pausing only to pull the grass back over the entrance, she zoomed back to school as fast as she could.

'I've been thinking about our project,' said Bimi at breakfast. Her blue eyes sparkled with excitement. 'We could do a tapestry.'

'Um . . . a tapestry?' Twink gazed at the oak-leaf platter of seed cakes with a worried frown. What did wasps eat, anyway?

'Yes, it'll be glimmery!' Bimi poured herself some fresh morning dew from the almond-shell pitcher. 'I thought we could do a sort of history of fairies. I mean, nothing brainy like Pix is doing – just a story in pictures, with lots of glitter and sparkle. What do you think?'

'Hmm? Oh! Yes, that sounds great.' Twink tried to look as if she had been listening to every word. Across the table, she saw Sooze drizzle honey on to her seed cakes. *Of course!* she thought with sudden relief. Wasps liked sweet things, didn't they?

Bimi's wings tapped together. 'Twink . . . is everything OK?'

Twink jumped, and nodded vigorously. 'Fine!'

Bimi gave her a funny look. 'You seem sort of distracted.'

'Oh, I'm just tired.' Twink's lavender wings fluttered as she gave a wide yawn. She didn't have to pretend much. She had only just managed to slip back into her bed before Mrs Hover came into Daffodil Branch to wake them all up.

'Oh.' Bimi looked down at her lap. 'Well . . . I just thought I'd tell you about my idea, that's all. I guess it's probably not very good.'

Feeling bad, Twink squeezed her friend's arm.

'No, it's great! Honestly, Bimi, a tapestry sounds like a wonderful idea. We'll have loads of fun doing it!'

A shy smile crept across Bimi's face. 'Do you really think it's a good idea? I mean, *really*?'

'Really!' Twink assured her warmly. 'It sounds completely glimmery! It'll be the best project of all, wait and see.'

Eyes shining, Bimi nibbled on her seed cake. 'Well, where do you think we can get the materials from? I thought Mrs Hover might be able to help . . .'

Twink tried to forget about the wasp as she chatted with Bimi about the tapestry. It wasn't easy. Her thoughts kept straying to him, alone and hurt in the old stump. Had he understood that she was coming back?

A river of brightly coloured butterflies swept into the Branch, stirring the air with their wings. Twink rose with the others, trying to look casual as the butterflies began clearing the tables. Pretending to finish her last swallow of dew, she hung back, heart pounding.

When she was sure no one was looking, she quickly grabbed the honey pot and tucked it into her petal bag. Slinging it over her shoulder, she flitted across to where Bimi stood with the others, queuing to take off. Phew! She had done it.

'Feeling hungry?' drawled a voice.

Chapter Three

Twink started. Mariella had sidled up beside her.

'I – I don't know what you mean!' gasped Twink.

Mariella raised a silvery-green eyebrow and looked at Twink's bag. 'Whatever. *I* don't care what you get up to. Why should I?' With a pointed smile, she turned away and whispered to Lola.

Bimi stared at them. 'What was *that* about?'

'Who knows!' Her face on fire, Twink pushed ahead and flew out into the trunk. Never mind, she told herself as they flew to their Creature Kindness class. Mariella could think whatever she liked. The important thing was that she had the honey for Stripe.

'Shall we go and talk to Mrs Hover during our free period?' said Bimi. 'She might have some scraps we could use for our tapestry.'

'Um – maybe later,' said Twink. 'There's something I've got to do.'

Bimi glanced at her in surprise. 'What?'

'I – oh, just something.' Twink felt a flush creep up her face.

'Oh.' Bimi looked hurt for a moment, and then shrugged. 'Well – maybe we can talk to her after dinner, then.'

'Great!' agreed Twink with relief. They landed in their Creature Kindness classroom.

Unlike the other teachers, Mr Woodleaf didn't have any drawings or decorations in his branch. Instead, it was filled with all sorts of animal paraphernalia, and even animals themselves. A large green moth sat on top of a bark cabinet, and a pair of grey woodlice lay curled up in a corner.

Twink and the others perched on their mushroom

seats, waiting for Mr Woodleaf to finish setting up their lesson. As this seemed to consist of coaxing four fidgeting ladybirds to stand in a straight line, it looked as if they'd be waiting for some time.

'Now, don't *you* wander off,' muttered Mr Woodleaf, prodding one of the insects back into place. At the same time, two more ladybirds trundled off across the table. The class giggled.

'Right,' said Mr Woodleaf finally, clearing his throat. He glanced nervously at his class. 'These are, um – some very worried ladybirds.'

Twink craned forward with the rest of the class to look at the bright red and black insects.

'See how they keep pacing, and trying to get away?' Mr Woodleaf licked his lips. His green hair stood on end like a hedgehog's spikes where he had run his hands through it. 'They're, ah – nervous wrecks, poor things.'

Twink held back a giggle. She thought Mr Woodleaf looked a bit of a nervous wreck himself! Everyone knew their Creature Kindness teacher was terrified of his students.

'What are they so worried about, sir?' asked Pix.

Mr Woodleaf swallowed, and rubbed his wings together. 'These ladybirds have all been captured by humans, and ah . . . told to fly away home, because their house is on fire and their children all gone.'

A stunned silence fell over the class. 'But – that's horrible!' cried Sili. 'Why would the humans *say* such a thing?'

'For a joke,' said Mr Woodleaf. He nodded grimly at their shocked expressions, and seemed to gain confidence. 'Humans have strange ideas sometimes! And now, these poor ladybirds are all convinced that if they don't keep racing home to check on their children, they'll lose them in flames.'

Twink stared at the fidgeting ladybirds. How awful! The poor ladybirds!

'But sir, how can we help them?' burst out Sooze. 'We can't just *leave* them like this!' The lavender-haired fairy's fists were clenched. She looked ready to fly at the first human she saw.

Mr Woodleaf paled and took a hasty step backwards. 'No, no, of course not!' he stammered. 'In cases like this, the first thing to try is a . . . a soothing song. And, ah – with any luck, they'll forget the terrible story they've been told.'

Fumbling in his pocket, Mr Woodleaf brought out a reed whistle and blew a comforting note. 'Now, then, girls – after me.' Turning to the ladybirds, he started to sing:

> *Oh, little ladybirds,*
> *Don't be blue,*
> *Your houses are safe,*
> *And your children too!*
> *Don't be nervous, don't feel sad,*
> *Dance and frolic – let's be glad!*

The class joined in enthusiastically, beating their wings in time as they chorused *'Don't be nervous! Don't feel sad!'*. Twink sang along with the others, watching the ladybirds eagerly.

The ladybirds' antennae perked up as they listened. Slowly, they stopped fidgeting and seemed to relax. One or two of them began to tap their feet along

with the music. By the time the fairies had sung the tune several times through, all four ladybirds were dancing on the table, flapping their wings merrily.

Mr Woodleaf stopped, a shy smile on his face. The class burst into applause. 'Well done, sir!' called Pix.

A ferocious blush swept up their teacher's face. 'Yes, well . . . you see how it works. Let's, ah – set the ladybirds free now!'

The class gathered at the window to wave goodbye. The bright red and black insects flitted

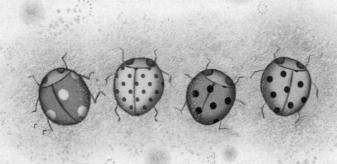

away without a care, dancing on the breeze.

'Glimmery!' breathed Twink. She and Bimi looked happily at each other.

Once they had all perched back on their mushrooms, Mr Woodleaf coughed for attention. 'Now, girls – the, ah, thing to remember is that similar creatures respond to similar treatments. So if you had another insect, a worried bee, for instance, or a nervous butterfly, you could calm it with the same sort of song.'

Twink's pointed ears pricked up. 'What about wasps?' she blurted out.

'*Wasps?*' Mr Woodleaf gaped as though he hadn't heard her right.

The room fell silent as everyone turned to stare at her. Mariella's eyes narrowed. Twink swallowed hard. 'Never mind,' she mumbled. 'I was just – thinking of something else.'

Mr Woodleaf shook his head. 'Yes. Well . . . let's continue, shall we? Who knows what to do about a grumpy earthworm? Zena?'

Twink's mind raced as the lesson went on. Similar

creatures responded to similar treatments! So if she could just find out how to heal an injured bee, then maybe she could help Stripe.

'Twink, you're not still thinking about that wasp, are you?' whispered Bimi. Her blue eyes were anxious.

'No, of course not.' Twink didn't look up. 'I was just curious, that's all.'

Bimi looked doubtful, but didn't say anything else. After class, Twink grabbed her things and flitted for the doorway. She had to get to the library!

To Twink's relief, the wasp ate the honey eagerly, licking the pot clean. Once finished, he touched Twink's hand with one of his thin legs and rubbed his stomach with another, his eyes shining with contentment.

'I'm glad you liked it!' laughed Twink. 'Now, let's do something about your wing.'

Opening the petal book she'd found in the library, Twink read the brief entry in *The Fairies' Guide to Helpful Insects* again, her pink eyebrows furrowed.

Bees rarely injure their wings, though sometimes the wings of older bees can become frayed with age. When this happens, a soothing salve of honeysuckle nectar, fresh morning dew and dried buttercup flower can be most effective when combined with a healing song.

Twink's mouth tightened worriedly. Stripe's wing was injured, not 'frayed with age'! Would the salve still work? And what sort of healing song, anyway?

'I guess I'll just make one up,' she decided.

Stripe's large eyes watched her as she carefully prepared the salve in an acorn bowl. The fresh morning dew had been easy to get, and with a bit of searching, she had found the other ingredients in the cupboard of her Flower Power classroom.

The mixture became a creamy paste as she stirred. Stripe peered into the bowl and sniffed it, his good wing fluttering with curiosity.

'Now for a healing song,' said Twink.

She thought for a moment, and then started smoothing the salve on to Stripe's broken wing. The wasp winced, but seemed to understand that he needed to keep still as Twink sang:

Heal, wing, heal!
Don't be broken, heal!
Mend together,
Whatever the weather.
Heal, wing, heal!

There was a flash of green light from the salve. Stripe jumped, and craned his neck to look over his shoulder. Twink sank back on to her heels, heart thumping. The salve glowed for a moment, and

then disappeared.

Stripe's wing was still broken.

'Oh!' breathed Twink in disappointment. Had her song not been good enough? Or had she mixed the salve wrong? But it had glowed! Surely that was a good sign?

Maybe the spell just took time to work. Twink gazed anxiously at Stripe's wing, trying to work out whether it was less crooked and bent than it had been. She couldn't tell. If only there was someone she could ask! Mr Woodleaf, or her parents, even.

Twink's spirits leapt as she thought of her mother and father. Her parents were the kindest, wisest fairies she knew – and as Fairy Medics, they dealt with poorly creatures all the time. They'd be sure to know how to help Stripe.

But what if they were just as horrified as everyone else? Twink winced at the thought. No, she couldn't ask them. She couldn't ask anyone.

'We'll just have to wait and see,' she murmured, stroking Stripe's back. 'I'll put more salve on tomorrow.'

The wasp nuzzled her hand with his head, humming worriedly.

Twink smiled. 'You can understand every word I say, can't you? Oh, it's so daft, Stripe – nobody could hate you once they *knew* you. But everyone just keeps talking about the Great Wasp Wars. Neither of us were even born then!'

Her head jerked up as a sudden noise came from outside the stump. Stripe stiffened and stared at the doorway. Frowning, Twink flitted to the door.

'Hello?' she called cautiously, peering out.

Nobody was there. The long strands of grass around the doorway waved gently, as though something had left in a hurry.

Twink swallowed as the blades of grass slowly stilled. *It was probably just a cricket,* she told herself. *That's all. Nothing to worry about.*

But even so, her wings felt as cold as ice.

Chapter
Four

The first-year Common Branch was a long, comfortable room with soft moss carpets. Glowworm lanterns dotted the ceiling, and a cluster of fire rocks glowed warm in the winter and cool in the summer. Now, in early autumn, the rocks gave off a friendly heat that the young fairies found very welcome.

Sitting at one of the mushroom desks, Twink tried to do her Flower Power homework – perking up a pot of drooping clover. But no matter what she tried, the round green leaves still sagged sadly.

Finally Twink sighed and pushed the acorn pot away. It was no use. You had to really concentrate to heal a plant, and all she could think of was Stripe, alone in his stump. *I hope he's not cold*, she thought, glancing at the dark windows.

Around her, the other first-year fairies chattered and worked on their projects. Everyone seemed to be having great fun with them. Even Bimi was busy, drawing on a piece of oak-leaf parchment.

'Watch, everyone!' called Sooze. 'This is my new dance!'

Twink looked up as Sooze leapt to the centre of the branch. Sili laughed. 'Go on, Sooze, impress us!'

'Right, here it is.' Sooze pushed her oak-leaf cap jauntily over one eye and then did a high kick that sent several fairies flitting backwards. Snapping her fingers, she strutted across the branch on the points of her toes, kicking with every step. Then with a sudden high leap she started twisting and spinning, shaking her hips and clapping her hands.

With a final prance, Sooze shot over their heads, pink wings fluttering. She drifted down to earth with a *whoop!* and punched the air.

'Well, what do you think?' she demanded.

The fairies had held back their laughter as Sooze danced, but now they erupted into shouts of merriment. 'Oh, Sooze!' gasped Pix, holding her sides. 'What kind of a dance is *that*?'

'A new one!' grinned Sooze. 'Madame will never have seen anything like it before.'

'Well, that's true – *nobody* has,' said Zena. She shook her head with an admiring smile. 'Sooze, you're too much!'

'Ha! You're all just jealous of my wonderful dancing skills!' Sooze plunged into her whirlwind dance again, snapping her fingers. Sili jumped up to join her, following her moves. The two girls collided midair, and collapsed into giggles.

Pix rolled her eyes. 'You two will get us into trouble if you're not careful! You know we're not supposed to fly in here.'

Sooze pulled Sili to her feet. 'Oh, stop worrying, Pix. Come on, Sili, let's do it again!'

Twink smiled as Sooze and Sili high-kicked their

way across the branch. Zena was right – Sooze was too much sometimes! And unlike Twink, she never seemed to have a care in the world. Twink turned back to her clover with a sigh.

But before she could get started on it again, Bimi came over, bouncing with excitement. 'Look, I've done a plan for our tapestry!' She held out the oak-leaf parchment. 'What do you think?'

Twink made room for Bimi on the mushroom seat, and the two fairies sat side by side, wings touching, as they looked at the parchment.

As Bimi had said, it showed the history of the fairies: kings and queens in old-fashioned clothing; Glitterwings as a tiny sapling; the Great Wasp Wars; Queen Mab as a young ruler. In the final drawings, Glitterwings had grown to a mighty tree, and Queen Mab sat wise and ancient on her fairy throne.

'Bimi, it's wonderful!' said Twink in surprise. Somehow she had half-believed her friend when she'd insisted she wouldn't do a good job.

Bimi ducked her head down with a shy smile. 'It's

not too bad, is it?'

'*Bi*-mi!' Twink flapped her wings, laughing. 'Weren't you listening? It's completely glimmery!'

Bimi's pretty face flushed with pleasure. 'And guess what – I asked Mrs Lightwing if we could do our project together, and she said yes! So I reckon we'll need to start sewing in all our spare time – during break, and our free periods, and maybe even a few lunches –'

Twink's heart sank to the floor. She needed all of her spare time to take care of Stripe. 'Bimi, I'm sorry, but . . . I can't,' she forced out.

Bimi's eyes widened. 'But I thought we were doing it together!'

Twink tried to laugh. 'You don't need me. Look how well you've done already! Besides, I – I've got an idea for a project of my own that I want to do.'

Hurt creased Bimi's face. 'But you said you'd help! Twink, please – I can't do it without you.'

'Of course you can!' cried Twink. Guilt pinched at her. 'You'll do a fantastic job, wait and see.'

Bimi slowly rose from the mushroom and tucked

the parchment under her arm.

'Bimi, I'm sorry,' said Twink miserably. 'I'd love to do the project with you. I just can't.'

Bimi stared at her. 'Why not?'

Twink faltered. In the middle of the branch, Sooze and Sili were still dancing noisily. Several of the others had joined in, too – including Pix, who had given up trying to keep order and was now kicking higher than anybody.

'I just can't, that's all.' Twink played with her snail-trail pen, unable to meet her friend's eyes. 'Like I said, there's something else I want to do, on my own.'

Bimi shrugged and looked away. 'Well . . . whatever. Have fun with your project, I suppose.'

'Bimi, wait!' Twink called after the blue-haired fairy as she flew from the branch. But it was too late. Bimi was gone.

Twink slumped her chin on her hands. Oh, and she and Bimi had been getting on so well this term, too! Last term they'd fallen out for days, because Bimi had been jealous of Twink's friendship with

Sooze. Now, just when that finally seemed sorted, this had to happen.

And there was nothing Twink could do to fix it. She couldn't abandon Stripe, and she could never explain to Bimi what she was *really* doing. Twink's eyes stung with unspilled tears.

'Oh, deary me. Having problems, are we?' cooed a voice.

Twink started. Mariella stood leaning against the desk, fluttering her pale green wings innocently.

'What do *you* want?' muttered Twink. She wiped her eyes with the back of her hand.

'Nothing,' said Mariella, widening her eyes. 'I just overheard your little tiff with Bimi, that's all. Such a shame, isn't it?'

'What is?' asked Twink warily.

Mariella flapped a wing. 'You know – when you can't do two things at once. *Wasps*, I really hate it when that happens!'

Twink's breath caught in her throat. *Wasps?* Did Mariella mean –

Lola sidled up beside Mariella, smirking. 'Yeah,

wasps,' she echoed. 'Or . . . just *one* wasp, maybe.'
She and Mariella looked at each other and
sniggered.

Twink jumped up and grabbed Mariella's arm.
'You know, don't you?' she whispered fiercely. 'You
found out, somehow!'

Mariella's green eyes widened until they looked
like they might pop out. 'Found out what? I can't
imagine what you mean. Lola, do *you* know what
she means?'

Lola shook her head, imitating Mariella's wide-

eyed expression.

Twink dropped her hand as she suddenly realised what had happened. 'It was you, wasn't it?' she demanded. 'Outside the stump this afternoon. You were spying on me!'

Mariella's eyebrows arched. 'Well, that's nothing compared to *you*! Stealing honey from the school, sneaking off into the wood, making friends with a *wasp* –'

'Shh!' Twink looked over her shoulder. The others were still dancing and laughing, not paying any attention to them. She clenched her fists. 'You – you won't tell, will you?'

Mariella folded her arms across her chest. 'I really feel it's my duty to,' she said primly. 'You're betraying the fairies, Twink. Have you even *thought* how ashamed your parents would be? Not to mention Miss Shimmery! Why, she'd probably expel you!'

Twink swallowed hard. Sickeningly, she knew that Mariella was right. Both her parents and Miss Shimmery would probably be horrified at what she had done.

'Please, Mariella,' she whispered. 'You can't tell! It's not just me, it's Stripe. He's hurt, and –'

Twink stopped as an expression of wicked delight burst across Mariella's face. '*Stripe?*' she repeated. 'You've given it a *name*? Oh, that's just glimmery!' She nudged Lola, and they dissolved into snorts and splutters.

Twink's face was on fire. 'Mariella, you can't tell!' she said desperately. 'Remember what happened last term? No one thinks much of tell-tales here!'

Mariella stopped laughing as a look of doubt crossed her face. She recovered herself with a sneer. 'It's not telling tales when it's this serious! You heard what Madame said – no fairy has helped a wasp for a thousand years. No one would ever forgive you, Twink. And they'd probably banish that wasp friend of yours – or worse!'

Twink's blood turned to ice. '*Please* don't tell, Mariella!' she begged.

'Hmm.' Propping her finger on her chin, Mariella tilted her head to one side in exaggerated consideration.

'Please!' said Twink again. She swallowed hard. 'I'll do anything you want!'

Mariella slowly dropped her finger. Her green eyes glinted like a flash of snakeskin.

'Anything?' she asked.

Chapter Five

Twink felt as if the next few days would never end. It seemed like every time she turned round, Mariella had another petty little chore for her to do: polishing her pixie boots, carrying her petal bag between classes, even doing her homework.

Twink had baulked at this last task. 'Mariella, I'm not going to do your homework for you!' she said hotly. 'That's cheating.'

The pointed-faced fairy had merely raised a silvery eyebrow. 'Oh. Well, I suppose you don't care about Stripe very much, do you?'

That was always her answer whenever Twink objected. And then Twink had no choice but to grit her teeth and do whatever horrid task Mariella had ordered. The only good thing was that everyone was so wrapped up in their projects that nobody had noticed she'd turned into Mariella's personal slave!

Even Bimi hadn't noticed – which wasn't too surprising, since her best friend seemed to be avoiding her. Every time Twink saw Bimi she was hard at work on her tapestry, keeping her blue head firmly down.

Twink had tried to talk to her a few times, but conversation between the two girls had become stiff and awkward. Finally Twink gave up. She ached to make things up with her friend, but how could she? She didn't dare tell Bimi about Stripe – Bimi hated wasps as much as everyone else!

Twink sighed as she wrote out Mariella's Fairy Dust homework. At least she knew now that the healing spell was working on Stripe. For over a week now, she had applied it faithfully – and to her immense joy, Stripe's wing had first straightened, and then started to mend itself.

It won't be much longer, she told herself fervently. *Stripe will be well soon, he really will!* Then she could let him go, and Mariella could say whatever she liked.

And maybe things could get back to normal with her and Bimi.

'Stripe, hold still!' laughed Twink. 'I've got to put the salve on.'

In answer, the young wasp rolled on to his back, wiggling his black legs in the air. Twink tickled his stomach and he hummed loudly, waving his legs about.

It was just before dawn: the hour when she and Stripe could spend the most time together. But Twink's nightly excursions were taking their toll. She had to fight to hold back her yawns during class, and had already been told off several times for not paying attention.

Mrs Lightwing had been especially scathing during Flight class yesterday, when Twink had bungled a series of barrel rolls.

'Great Mab, girl, are you *trying* to look like a bird in a hurricane?' their year Head had demanded, propping her hands on her hips. 'Because you're giving an excellent imitation of it!'

Stripe flipped over on to his front again. His large eyes gleamed in the light of the glow-worm lantern. The battered old stump felt cosy to them both now – a friendly, homely place.

'You're feeling better, aren't you!' grinned Twink. Holding the lantern up, she peered carefully at his wings. You had to look hard now to see that one of them was still slightly bent and torn.

'Glimmery!' she said happily. 'I bet you could fly *now*. But we'll put the salve on one more time, just to make sure. OK?' She tapped Stripe on the head with mock severity.

The wasp settled down. Twink smoothed the salve on to his wing with gentle fingertips as she sang in her high, sweet voice. Closing his eyes, Stripe swayed to the music.

A green flash lit Twink's face as the salve glowed briefly, and then vanished. Grabbing up the lantern, Twink eagerly scrutinised Stripe's wing.

'It's healed!' she cried. She scooped the wasp up into a hug. 'Oh, Stripe, it looks as good as new! You can fly now, I'm sure of it!'

Stripe twisted about in astonishment, staring at his wing over his shoulder. He fluttered it, testing it out.

Twink leapt from the bed and darted across the room. 'Come on!' she cried. 'Fly to me!'

Stripe's eyes widened. He hesitated, not moving.

'What's wrong?' said Twink. 'Come on, you can do it!'

The wasp looked anxious. His legs moved restlessly, as though he was about to take off.

Twink clapped her hands. 'That's it! Just jump into the air!'

Stripe seemed to take a big breath. All at once, he crouched his black legs and jumped. He seemed to hang in the air for a moment, his wings not moving . . . and then he crashed to the floor.

'Oh!' gasped Twink. She raced to his side. The little wasp sat up, looking dazed. 'Stripe, what happened?' she asked, stroking his back. 'You didn't even *try* to move your wings!'

The wasp's eyes filled with tears. He huddled against the floor, looking miserable.

Twink stared at him. 'Stripe? What's wrong?' But then all at once she knew. 'You're . . . you're scared, aren't you?' she said slowly.

Stripe looked away. Twink sat cross-legged beside him. 'Is it because of whatever happened to you?' she asked in a hushed voice. 'Has it made you afraid to fly again?'

Stripe sighed. He had no way of telling Twink

about the magpie that had attacked him, or the nightmares that had haunted him ever since. No matter how he tried, he couldn't forget the terror of tumbling through the air, unable to fly.

'I know whatever happened must have been really scary, but your wings are fine now,' Twink reassured him. 'And you need to fly again, so you can go home to your family. I bet they miss you!'

Stripe listened intently to her, his large eyes taking in every word. At the mention of his family, he took a deep breath and stood up, fluttering his wings again.

'That's it!' Twink jumped up. 'Come on, fly to me.' She backed away a few steps and held out her hands.

Stripe's mouth was set in determination. His wings buzzed louder and louder, faster and faster, until they became a white blur. Any moment now, he'd take off! Twink watched him, hardly daring to breathe.

Stripe lifted off the floor. Immediately, panic crossed his face. His legs scrambled frantically for a

foothold as his wings faltered and stopped. Twink just managed to jump forward and catch him before he fell again.

'Oh, Stripe,' she said sadly. She carried him back to the bed. He crawled away to the battered old pillow and hid his head.

He looked so miserable that Twink felt her own eyes fill with tears. 'I'm sorry,' she said. 'It was all my fault!'

Stripe peeped out with a quizzical frown.

Twink nodded earnestly. 'If anyone should know what it's like to be scared of flying, it's me! It was stupid of me to push you so soon. I acted like a real –' She stopped, the word *wasp brain* catching in her throat. 'I – I acted really stupidly,' she finished lamely.

Stripe stared at her in surprise. He crawled on to her lap and peered into her face, his eyes asking a question.

'It's true,' said Twink. She told the wasp how she had been too scared to fly during her first term at Glitterwings, and how awful it had been for her.

'But I got over it, and so will you, Stripe.' She patted his head. 'You really will, I promise. Just keep trying!'

That evening Twink sat in the cosy warmth of the Common Branch, doodling on her petal pad as she did her homework. How could she help Stripe? Somehow, she had to show him that he *could* fly – even if he thought he was too scared!

Lost in thought, Twink hardly noticed when Mariella and Lola flitted into the room.

The other first-year fairies – most of them hard at work on their projects – raised their eyebrows at each other. Those two hardly ever came into the Common Branch. Mariella could never resist sneering at everything around her, and the jibes that this brought on from Sooze and the others usually had everyone rolling about in fits of laughter – making Mariella look extremely silly! As a result, she and Lola normally kept out of the Common Branch altogether.

'Are you going to behave yourself tonight, Mariella?' asked Sooze with a glint in her violet eyes. 'Or are we going to have to give you the usual treatment?'

Mariella sniffed and tossed her silvery-green hair. 'I don't know what you mean! Lola and I have just come in to do our homework. Is that allowed?'

Pix grinned. 'It's allowed. Just make sure that's all you do!'

Mariella and Lola went to a pair of spotted mushroom desks and sat side by side, whispering behind their wings as they did their homework. Everyone went back to their own projects, and gradually the buzz of conversation returned to its usual level.

Then, during a brief lull, Mariella yawned and stretched, fluttering her wings. 'I'm thirsty,' she announced loudly. 'Twink, go and fetch me some fresh morning dew, will you?'

Twink's head jerked up from her petal pad. Her cheeks caught fire as she realised everyone was staring. *I'm already doing your homework for you!* she thought. *Isn't that enough?*

Obviously it wasn't. Mariella sat watching her, her eyes wide and innocent.

'Listen to you!' scoffed Sooze, flapping her pink wings. 'Do you think Twink's your servant or something?'

Mariella looked hurt. 'I'm just asking her to get me some fresh dew, that's all. I'm sure she doesn't mind. Do you, Twink?'

Of course I mind! Get your own dew! Twink wanted to shout. Then she thought of Stripe, and forced a laugh. 'No, I don't mind. Does – does anybody else want some?'

Sooze propped her hands on her hips. 'Twink, you're not actually going to *get* it for her!'

'I was just about to go and stretch my wings anyway.' Twink stood up, trying to sound casual. She could see Mariella smirking from the corner of her eye. Oh, she was loving this!

'Yes, but . . .' Pix trailed off, looking completely baffled. She stared from Twink to Mariella and back again.

Twink gulped. The whole branch was gaping at her like she had lost her mind. Her friends would realise something was up if she didn't think fast! She glanced at Bimi. Her best friend was sitting on the floor working on her tapestry, watching Twink with a strange expression on her face.

The tapestry! Twink felt a rush of relief as an idea came to her. 'Don't you get it, everyone? This is my project!' she said brightly.

Sooze's eyes narrowed. 'What? Fetching dew for Mosquito Nose?'

Twink's pink hair tumbled about her face as she shook her head. 'No – making new friends! Trying to get on with people that I haven't got on with before. It's for the betterment of the school, just like Miss Shimmery said!'

There was a pause.

'I'm – I'm going to write a report on it, and maybe even a song about friendship – it's going to be completely glimmery!' said Twink in a rush. 'I bet I'll even get a sparkle mark!'

She held her breath as the other fairies looked at each other.

'Oh,' said Pix finally. She blinked. 'Well, that's . . . original.'

Mariella stifled a yawn behind her hand. 'Twink, where's that dew?' she called. 'I really am getting *terribly* thirsty.'

Lola sniggered. Heat rushed to Twink's cheeks as she flitted to the doorway.

Sooze shook her head in disgust. 'You're mad, Twink,' she said flatly. 'All this for a sparkle mark! Why not just throttle Mariella? That would *really* be for the betterment of the school!'

Chapter
Six

Twink had worried that Mariella would show her up again that evening, but once the fairies were all back in Daffodil Branch, Sooze and Sili started a flying pillow fight that soon had everyone screaming with laughter. Nobody would have noticed Mariella if she'd stood on a bed and shouted out her orders!

'Take that, Opposite!' shrieked Sooze, zooming up towards the ceiling as she threw a cotton-bud pillow at Twink. She missed, hitting Zena instead.

'Oh!' Zena scooped up the pillow and hurled it back at Sooze, who darted nimbly out of the way.

The pillow smacked one of the daffodil canopies, and Sili did a midair somersault and grabbed it, walloping it back at Zena.

'We're going to get into trouble!' shouted Pix, skimming from one end of the branch to the other. 'Everyone, stop! We're going to – oof!' A pillow hit her in the mouth. 'All right, you asked for it!' she laughed, grabbing it off the floor and entering the fray.

Twink laughed and shouted with the others, flinging pillows until Mrs Hover appeared in the doorway.

'I never!' she huffed, flapping her wings. 'Are you first-year students at Glitterwings Academy, or babies in an acorn nursery? I want to see hair brushed and wings polished this instant, and all of you in bed in five minutes flat!'

The girls flitted to their bedside mushrooms, still giggling. Twink sat on her moss bed and worked her thistle comb through her dishevelled hair.

'Twink, can I talk to you?' whispered Bimi. The blue-haired fairy hadn't really joined in with the others, and now her expression looked earnest and worried.

Twink nodded quickly, putting down her comb. 'Of course!'

Bimi hesitated. 'I – I'm sorry about the way I've been acting,' she said. 'I was hurt that you're not doing the tapestry with me, but –' She stopped, looking at Twink closely.

'What?' whispered Twink, her heart pounding.

'But something's wrong, isn't it?' said Bimi. She sat down beside Twink, her eyes grave. 'Twink, I know your project isn't *really* making friends with Mariella! What's going on?'

Twink glanced over her shoulder. Mariella and Lola sat apart from the others as usual. Lola was busy plaiting her pale, wispy hair, and Mariella had her nose in the air, polishing her wings with the expensive lotion her mother had sent her.

Twink swallowed. 'I – I can't tell you.'

Bimi's expression fell. 'Oh, Twink! Is it because I acted like such a wasp brain over the tapestry? I'm really sorry about that. You can trust me, I promise!'

On Twink's bedside mushroom, the drawings of her family smiled out at her – her parents, and Teena, her little sister. Twink sighed. What would they think about this mess?

'No, it's not that.' She cleared her throat. 'It's – it's something that I can't tell anyone.'

Bimi rubbed her silver and gold wing against Twink's lavender one. 'You're not in some kind of trouble, are you?'

Twink stared down at her comb. Part of her longed to tell Bimi everything – but how could she? She knew how Bimi felt about wasps.

'Bedtime, girls!' announced Mrs Hover, bustling heavily about the branch. 'Under the covers now, flitter-flutter!'

Bimi reluctantly returned to her own bed, slipping under her yellow-petal duvet. 'Twink, whatever it is, you can tell me,' she whispered. 'I want to help.'

Twink hesitated. 'I can't. I can't tell anyone.'

A hurt look crossed Bimi's face. 'But I'm your best friend.'

'I know, but – but it's something I just can't talk about,' mumbled Twink. She climbed under the covers of her own bed, not looking at Bimi.

'But –'

'I just can't, all right?' whispered Twink. 'Leave me alone!' She flopped over on to her side, clutching her petal duvet around her miserably.

'Glow-worms out!' called Mrs Hover. The branch plunged into darkness, lit only by the moonlight streaking in from the window. Twink lay awake for a long time, listening for a sound from the bed next to her.

But Bimi didn't ask again.

As the night slowly turned to dawn, Twink flew into Miss Petal's classroom. She was quite used now to the shadowy, empty branch, and she flew quickly to the broken window. Tucking the pot of honey under one arm, she eased the latch open and started to clamber through.

'Where are you going?' demanded a voice.

Stifling a shriek, Twink swung round in the air.

Bimi hovered in the classroom doorway, wearing her nightclothes.

'What are *you* doing here?' cried Twink.

Bimi flitted into the room, stopping a wing's breadth from Twink. 'I couldn't sleep. I was worried about you. Then I heard you get up and sneak out – so I followed you.'

Her eyes fell on the honey under Twink's arm. 'What's that?'

'Nothing!' Red-faced, Twink whisked it behind her back. 'Bimi, go back to bed! I'll tell you what's going on later, but – but I can't now.'

Bimi folded her arms across her chest. 'Are you mad? I'm not going anywhere! And if *you* try to go somewhere without me, I'll fly straight to Mrs Lightwing!'

Twink stared at her in dismay. 'But I thought you were my friend,' she whispered.

'I *am* your friend!' cried Bimi. 'And friends don't turn their backs when a friend's in trouble. Now, are we both going to go to wherever-it-is – or are we just going to fly back to bed?'

Twink swallowed. *How* could she let Bimi see Stripe? But he was waiting for her, expecting his breakfast. She had to go to him.

'OK, we'll go,' she muttered finally. Her heart felt like a stone. 'But, Bimi –' She stopped. *Please still be my friend. Please don't hate me for helping a wasp!*

Bimi touched her arm. 'What?'

'Never mind.' Looking away, Twink tucked in her wings and squeezed through the window. 'Come on, then, if you're coming.'

The night wind whispered through their wings as they flew around the back of the school. They came to the little dell, and Bimi's eyes widened.

'Isn't this where we found that old stump cottage?'

'That's right,' said Twink glumly. She swooped down and hovered in front of the long blades of grass that covered its door. 'And – and that's where we're going.'

Bimi flew down beside her. 'Is something in there?' she breathed, peering into the gloom.

Before Twink could answer, a buzzing noise came from inside the stump. Bimi stiffened. 'Oh, Twink! It's not a –'

Twink bit her lip and darted inside. 'Glow-worm on,' she said to the lantern that hung near the ceiling. Immediately, a cheerful light filled the worn little room.

Twink gasped. Stripe was sitting on the table! How on earth had he got there?

When Stripe saw her, he gave a little hop, fluttering his wings. Suddenly he lifted into the air. His wings wobbled a bit . . . but he was flying!

Forgetting Bimi, Twink ran to the wasp and scooped him up in a hug.

'Oh, Stripe!' she cried. 'I knew you could do it!' He hummed happily, nestling into her arms.

'A – a wasp,' whispered Bimi. Twink turned. Her friend had followed her inside, and now her face was as pale as snow. Bimi backed away towards the door.

Twink flitted over to her. 'Bimi, Stripe was hurt, and he called to me. I couldn't just ignore him! And – and look how sweet he is.' She held the wasp out to her friend.

Bimi stared at the wasp without moving. 'What do you mean, he called to you? Wasps can't do magic!'

Twink shook her head. 'I don't know. He hasn't done it since. But he really did call to me. And then when I found him, his wing was horribly broken. I couldn't just leave him in the wood!'

Bimi didn't say anything.

Twink rushed on, 'So – so I brought him here. And I managed to heal his wing, but he's been too

scared to fly – until now, you clever thing!' she added to Stripe, nuzzling his fur with her nose.

'And Mariella found out, didn't she?' guessed Bimi. Flitting over to one of the spotted mushroom stools, she sank down with a sigh. 'Oh, Twink! Why did you have to get involved with a *wasp*?'

Stripe grew very still, staring at Bimi. Twink knew his feelings were hurt, and her wings stiffened. 'I told you, he was injured!' she snapped. 'And don't say *wasp* in that sneery way – maybe he's a wasp, but he's nicer than some fairies I know.'

For a moment she and Bimi glared at each other. Then Stripe pulled himself out of Twink's arms and flew shakily across to Bimi, landing with a *plop* on the mushroom table in front of her.

Bimi gave a shriek. 'Oh! Get it away from me!' She shrank back in her chair, too frightened to move.

Stripe crept across the table until he was next to her. Slowly, he touched Bimi's arm with one of his thin black legs. Twink held her breath as the two of them gazed at each other, still as statues.

Finally Bimi swallowed. 'He – he has very big eyes, doesn't he?' she said weakly.

Twink came over to them. 'His fuzz is really soft, too,' she offered.

Bimi moved her hand towards Stripe's back, and then jerked it back again. 'He won't sting me, will he?'

'Of course not!' Twink assured her. 'He's as friendly as you are.'

Bimi took a deep breath and tried again. When her hand rested on Stripe's back, she gasped in surprise. 'Oh – it's like a caterpillar's fur!' She stroked the wasp gently as he hummed.

Twink sat down on the other mushroom, propping her elbows on the table. 'Do you see, Bimi? I couldn't have just left him there.'

Bimi's cheeks reddened. 'No, I suppose you couldn't have. That was stupid of me. I'm sorry, Stripe,' she added to the wasp. He pushed against her hand with his head, and Bimi smiled.

Her expression grew serious again as she looked back at Twink. 'But what are we going to do about Mariella? If she tells – oh, Twink, it would be awful! You might even get expelled!'

'I know,' said Twink softly. The same thought had kept her awake countless times since she had met Stripe. Then she brightened. 'But Stripe's started flying again. I'm sure he'll be able to go home to his family soon. Then Mariella can say what she likes – if there's no wasp here, she can't prove it!'

'Maybe he could fly home now, if we helped him,' said Bimi eagerly. She leaned towards the wasp. 'Stripe, would you like to fly home to your family this morning?'

Stripe's eyes widened. He gulped, and beat his wings without taking off. He looked petrified and excited, both at the same time.

'Let's give him some practice!' Twink flew across to the bed. Landing lightly on top of it, she clapped her hands. 'Come on, Stripe, fly to me.'

The wasp took a deep breath. Launching himself in the air, he wobbled across the room in fits and spurts. At the last moment he crashed into Twink, and they fell on to the bed in a tangled heap.

Twink sat up and laughed. 'Well – almost!'

Bimi jumped on to her mushroom. 'Now back to me, Stripe!' she called.

Over and over, the wasp flew back and forth between the two fairies. Shaky at first, his flying gradually improved until he hardly wobbled at all.

'Stripe, that's brilliant!' said Twink. She stooped down to look into his eyes. 'Would – would you like to fly home now?' A painful lump grew in her throat at the thought. She tried to ignore it. She'd miss Stripe, but she knew he needed to be with his parents.

Stripe looked uncertain. He stared out of the door at the lightening sky and buzzed anxiously to himself.

'Maybe he needs a bit more practice,' said Bimi. 'Why don't we come back at break this afternoon and see him off then?'

'What do you think, Stripe?' asked Twink, stroking his back. 'Do you want to spend this morning practising? You could even try flying outside for a bit! Then when we come back we can say a proper goodbye to you.'

Stripe flew up into her arms, beating his wings gently against her chin. Twink hugged him in relief. She didn't have to say goodbye to her friend just yet.

'I think that's a yes,' laughed Bimi. 'All right, Stripe – you keep practising, and we'll see you off in style this afternoon!'

Chapter
Seven

At breakfast that morning Twink ate her seed cakes happily, enjoying the crunchy treat for the first time in what seemed like ages. Everything was going to be all right. She and Bimi were friends again – and Stripe was almost ready to return to his family!

Once breakfast was over, Twink rose with the others to queue for the door. 'Oh, there's Mrs Hover!' cried Bimi. 'I just want to ask her about some more glitter for my tapestry.'

As Bimi flitted off, Mariella edged over, fluttering her pale green wings innocently. 'Speaking of projects, Twink, what are you going to do for mine?'

Twink stared at her. '*Yours?*'

Mariella widened her eyes. 'Well, they're due tomorrow. And I *know* that you'll want to help me out with mine – won't you?'

Twink felt her jaw drop. 'You're mad! I'm not doing your project for you. I haven't even thought about *my* project yet!'

'Oh, but I thought you were doing that really glimmery project on friendship,' piped up Lola, her eyes shining meanly.

'Yes, that's right,' said Mariella. 'You've got *your* project all sorted, but you don't want to help me with mine! I call that selfish.'

'So do I,' echoed Lola, crossing her thin arms across her chest.

'And I think selfish people deserve whatever happens to them,' continued Mariella, narrowing her eyes. 'Especially ones with *secrets*.'

Twink's wings felt hot. 'I don't care!' she burst out. 'You can do whatever you like, Mariella. I'm not doing your project for you.'

Mariella gaped at her. '*What?*'

Twink gulped, but went on, 'You heard me. And – and you'd better think twice before you tell anyone about Stripe. You know what they think of tell-tales here!'

She flew off without waiting for a response, but not before she had seen the flash of anger in Mariella's eyes. Oh, wasps, she had really done it now!

Bimi fluttered back over, and the two friends flew out into the trunk together, spiralling upwards towards their Fairy Dust class. In a low voice, Twink told Bimi what had happened.

'The horrid thing!' exclaimed Bimi. 'She thinks she can make you do whatever she likes now, doesn't she?'

'Do you think she'll tell?' asked Twink anxiously. She glanced over her shoulder. Mariella and Lola were flying some way behind the others, whispering with their heads close together.

Bimi thought for a moment, and then shook her blue head. 'Not yet. I bet you've got her worried

about being a tell-tale – she'll want to plan it out really carefully before she says anything, and Stripe will probably be gone by then. It'll be fine, Twink, really!'

Banking sharply, they landed with a running skip on the ledge of their Fairy Dust classroom. Twink let out a breath. She hoped with all her heart that Bimi was right.

As the day went on and nothing happened, Twink's spirits lifted. She threw an excited glance at Bimi as they sat in their Creature Kindness class. Afternoon break was next! In just a few minutes, they'd be skimming down to the stump to say goodbye to Stripe.

'So . . . ah . . . that's how you calm down an angry ant,' mumbled Mr Woodleaf at the front of the branch. On the mushroom table, a large black ant lay on its back sniffing a daisy, looking the very picture of bliss.

'What if you don't have a daisy, sir?' called Pix.

Before Mr Woodleaf could respond, the magpie's

call echoed through the school, signalling the end of class. Breaktime! Twink jumped up with the other fairies, grabbing her things.

'Bluebell blossoms!' cried Mr Woodleaf over the bustle. 'Or – or sometimes orange leaf will work –'

Suddenly the fairies stopped, their eyes widening. 'What's that?' said Sooze.

The magpie's usual long call had changed to a series of short, piping bursts that rang through the school. Twink's fingers tightened on her petal bag. What was going on?

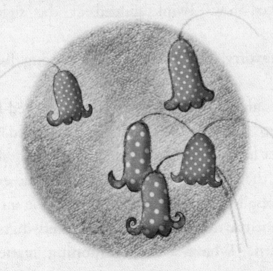

Mr Woodleaf let out a yelp and raked his fingers through his hair. 'We're being summoned to the Great Branch! Come on, girls, quickly – there must be some sort of emergency.'

With subdued whispers, the Daffodil Branch fairies flew into the trunk. Twink felt cold as she spiralled downwards.

Swooping into the Great Branch, she and Bimi flew to their usual seats at the Daffodil Branch table. Miss Shimmery stood waiting for the school to sit down. Behind her, all the year heads sat in a stony-faced row. Twink gulped at the sight of them.

'Don't worry!' whispered Bimi, squeezing Twink's hand.

Twink glanced at Mariella. The pointed-faced fairy gazed coolly back at her. Twink looked away again, her heart pounding hard.

When the Great Branch was full of silent, expectant fairies, Miss Shimmery lifted into the air and hovered before them. 'Students of Glitterwings,' she announced. 'I have a very distressing matter to discuss. I received an anonymous note this morning.'

Twink sat frozen to her mushroom. The twinkle that usually hid deep in the HeadFairy's eyes was nowhere to be seen.

'Normally I would ignore an anonymous note,' said Miss Shimmery. 'They're a tool for cowards. But the news contained in this one is most disturbing if it is true, and I cannot disregard it.'

Miss Shimmery pulled out a crumpled pink petal and unfolded it. '*Dear Miss Shimmery. We think you*

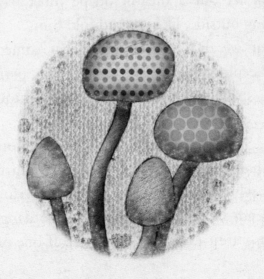

should know that a Glitterwings student has hidden an injured wasp in the old stump behind the school, and that she goes to see it every day,' she read out.

The school sat utterly still. Not a single wing flickered as the fairies stared at Miss Shimmery, horror written on their faces.

Twink swallowed hard.

The HeadFairy slowly refolded the note. 'You see why I cannot ignore this,' she said. 'Naturally, myself and all the year heads immediately went to the old stump. We didn't find a wasp –'

Twink let out a breath. Stripe must have been practising outside, like she had told him.

'– but we did find evidence that someone has been keeping *something* there, and performing healing spells on it.' A gasp rippled through the school.

Miss Shimmery's face was more serious than Twink had ever seen it. 'Now, I'm certain that the student who has done this thinks she's performing a good deed, but she doesn't realise the danger she's in. Wasps are treacherous creatures. If one of you is still hiding it, I must ask you to step forward immediately.'

Nobody moved. The fairies glanced uneasily at each other, wondering who among them was harbouring a wasp.

Twink could feel her friends staring at her in alarm. She looked down at the mossy table, her cheeks hot.

'Twink,' whispered Pix. 'That wasp we heard in Dance class – you didn't . . .' She trailed off.

On the platform, Miss Shimmery tapped her wings together. 'I would rather not resort to using magic to find out the truth,' she said firmly. 'That is not how we do things at Glitterwings.'

Twink trembled on her mushroom. She knew she had to confess, but how could she? Her parents would be horrified! And what if Stripe wasn't ready to fly home yet – what would happen to him?

'I will not ask again,' said Miss Shimmery.

Twink's heart felt like it was being gripped by a giant fist. Slowly, her legs shaking, she rose to her feet.

'Yes, Twink?' said Miss Shimmery gravely.

Twink's throat felt like dust. 'I . . .'

'A wasp!' screamed someone. Twink whirled to face the windows. There was Stripe, scrabbling in a panic at the glass! Then a robin swooped closely behind him, its beak open . . . and Stripe vanished from view.

Chapter
Eight

'Stripe!' shouted Twink. She flew for the window without thinking, wrenching it open and flinging herself outside. Stripe clung to a nearby branch, his sides heaving. The bird was poised above him, just about to strike.

'Leave him alone!' Twink screamed at the robin. She flew at it in a frenzy, shoving its red breast with both hands. The red and brown bird backed away in alarm as the entire school crowded at the windows, gaping at the scene.

'Sit down!' bellowed Miss Shimmery's voice.

'Girls! Sit down immediately!'

The robin took off in a flurry of feathers. Twink landed quickly beside the terrified wasp. He was hanging on to the rough bark with all six legs, but as Twink soothed him, he slowly crept into her lap and hid his face.

'Oh, Stripe,' whispered Twink, stroking him. 'What happened? Were you practising flying outside?'

'Twink,' said Miss Shimmery.

Twink looked up. The HeadFairy was hovering in front of her, her rainbow wings glinting in the sunshine.

'We must talk,' she said.

'But I *can't* take him back to the wood and just leave him there!' cried Twink. She held Stripe tightly in her arms as she stood in the HeadFairy's office. 'He's just a baby, and now he's too scared to fly again – anything could happen to him!'

'I'm sorry, Twink, but he must go back.' Miss Shimmery sat behind a broad mushroom desk, her wings folded behind her back. Drawings of the school in the different seasons hung on the walls around her.

Mrs Lightwing sat to one side, looking grim. 'Great Mab, girl, what were you thinking? A wasp, of all things!' She shook her sky-blue head.

'Can't we at least wait until he's not so scared?' begged Twink. Stripe clung to her, his eyes wide.

Miss Shimmery rose from her seat. 'No, Twink. He must go back now. I'm sure his family will find him.'

But what if they didn't? Twink couldn't speak. She buried her face in Stripe's furry back as tears burned in her eyes.

She felt Miss Shimmery's hand on her shoulder. 'Twink, I know we must seem very harsh to you. This is for the best, believe me – for Stripe, too, as well as for you and the school.'

Mrs Lightwing nodded firmly. 'That's right. Fairies and wasps don't mix – never have, never will!'

Twink's heart felt too heavy to fly, but somehow she managed the flight back to the wood, holding Stripe closely as Miss Shimmery and Mrs Lightwing flew on either side of her.

The trees closed around them as they entered the wood. 'This – this is the place,' choked out Twink finally. She pointed at the fallen log.

'Very well,' said Miss Shimmery. 'You may say goodbye now, Twink.'

Gulping back tears, Twink landed on the damp earth and carefully put Stripe down. 'Oh, Stripe, please be all right!' she said. 'Try calling out to your family, the way you called out to me.'

Stripe nuzzled against her hand. Twink stroked his head, unable to speak.

'Now, Twink,' said Miss Shimmery.

Swallowing hard, Twink dropped a quick kiss on Stripe's head. 'Goodbye,' she whispered. 'I – I hope I'll see you again someday.'

Swiftly, Twink flew back to her teachers.

'Come along,' said Miss Shimmery. 'He'll be all right. Wasps take care of their own.'

Twink longed to look behind her as they flew away, but knew she'd burst into tears if she did. She flew along miserably, hating herself.

As Glitterwings Academy came back into view, Twink couldn't bear it any longer. She stopped, and took a deep breath. 'I'm sorry, but – but I have to go back. He's only a baby, and he's scared.'

Mrs Lightwing looked thunderous. 'You'll do nothing of the sort, my girl! Wasps are devious creatures! They –'

A strange expression crossed Miss Shimmery's face. She laid a restraining hand on Mrs Lightwing's arm. 'Twink . . . do you really care so much for this wasp?'

Twink nodded. 'He's my friend,' she said in a small voice. 'I know fairies and wasps were at war once, but – but it doesn't seem to matter. Right now he's scared and confused, and I have to help him.'

'Extraordinary,' murmured Miss Shimmery. 'Twink, no fairy has been a friend of a wasp in a thousand years. I don't know what to think. I can't let you return to him if you're in any danger, but –'

Suddenly a loud barking filled the air. The three fairies swung about in surprise as a brown and white

terrier bounded across the grass.

Dogs were one of the few creatures who didn't understand that fairies were the helpers of nature. Instead they saw fairies as the most exciting game in the world, and loved to chase them if they could.

The terrier leapt into the air, snapping playfully at them. Distantly, Twink could hear a human calling, 'Jock? Jock, where are you?'

'Oh!' cried Miss Shimmery as the dog's teeth nipped one of her wings.

Twink gasped in horror as Miss Shimmery fell to the ground. Without thinking, she plunged into a dive to help the HeadFairy – and then shrieked and darted away as the dog jumped at her, white teeth snapping.

'Get back, you canine menace!' bellowed Mrs Lightwing, swatting the dog on the nose. It blinked in confusion.

Below, Miss Shimmery struggled to her feet. One of her wings was torn. 'Both of you fly back to school – hurry!' she called. 'Don't worry about me!'

The dog barked happily. Obviously deciding this

was some new game, it raced towards Miss Shimmery. In another moment it would trample her!

'No!' shouted Twink. She flew after it, yanking hard on its white tail. The dog whirled about in surprise. A big doggy grin burst across his face as he saw her.

'Ruff!' He started chasing his tail as fast as he could.

'Agh!' screamed Twink, hanging on for dear life. Her pink hair streamed behind her as the dog ran in faster and faster circles. Suddenly it stopped short, catapulting Twink through the air. A flock of midges scattered as she tumbled past.

'Oof!' Twink collided with Mrs Lightwing, and the two of them crashed to the ground beside Miss Shimmery. Twink rubbed her head, too stunned to fly.

'Get away! Hurry!' cried Miss Shimmery.

Mrs Lightwing pulled at Twink's arm. 'Get up, you foolish girl!'

'Come on!' Twink heard a fairy shout from the

direction of the school. 'A dog's got them!'

Twink's wings felt frozen. The terrier's face filled the sky as it danced about, snapping at the three fairies. It lunged towards Twink, its teeth glinting.

Suddenly a blur of yellow and black sped through the air.

'Arroooo!' wailed the terrier as the wasp stung it on the nose. It shook its head, trying desperately to rid itself of the invader, but was merely stung again for its efforts. Howling in pain, the dog turned tail and raced back to its owner.

'Stripe!' breathed Twink. The little wasp landed next to her, humming happily. She hugged him hard. 'Stripe, you saved us!'

Miss Shimmery and Mrs Lightwing stood staring, their mouths open. Closing them abruptly, they looked at each other in amazement.

Stripe tugged at Twink's arm, pointing upwards. Looking up, Twink saw two adult wasps hovering overhead. 'Your parents found you!' she cried. 'Oh, Stripe, that's glimmery!'

All at once Twink saw the other fairies. It looked

as if the whole school had sped out to help them, and now they all hovered a little distance away – hundreds of fairies in bright flower-dresses, watching in wonder. Twink caught Bimi's eye, and the two fairies smiled at each other.

Stripe's parents dipped down until they were buzzing in front of Miss Shimmery. Reaching out a leg, one of them touched her injured wing with concern. Fairy and wasp looked into each other's eyes for a moment.

Miss Shimmery inclined her head. 'I'll be fine,

thank you,' she said. 'And please thank your son for helping us.'

With a satisfied nod, the two wasps turned to Stripe.

'Goodbye, Stripe,' Twink whispered. 'I'll miss you!' Stripe nestled against her. Then Twink opened her arms, and he flew back to join his parents.

The three wasps hovered above for a moment. Stripe's parents dipped their wings to Twink, saying *thank you* with their eyes. And then they were all away, skimming off towards the wood.

Twink stared after them. Miss Shimmery stood beside her, watching as the wasps disappeared from view.

Finally the HeadFairy cleared her throat. 'Well, Twink . . . I'm not entirely sure what to do with you. I think you must have broken every rule that we have.'

Twink licked dry lips. 'Will – will I be expelled?

She held her breath as Miss Shimmery glanced at Mrs Lightwing. For a moment, Twink thought she saw a brief smile play across the HeadFairy's lips.

But then it was gone, and Twink knew she must have imagined it.

'I'm not sure what we'll do yet, Twink.' Miss Shimmery looked towards the wood with a thoughtful frown. 'I'll have to consider the matter carefully, and discuss it with Mrs Lightwing and your parents.'

Her parents! Twink felt the blood fall from her face.

'Come on now, girl,' said Mrs Lightwing gruffly. 'It's time to get back to school.'

That night the first-year fairies clustered about Twink in the Common Branch, clamouring to know everything. Twink told the story as best she could, with Bimi adding bits here and there. When she had finished, there was silence.

'That's . . . the most amazing story I've ever heard,' said Sooze finally.

Pix nodded earnestly. 'Twink, I never thought *anyone* could trust a wasp. But you two were really friends, weren't you? We all saw how he saved you.'

'Well, I'm just glad you didn't listen to us!' exclaimed Sili, fluttering her wings. 'The poor thing – he might have died if you hadn't helped him.'

Twink smiled with relief. Her friends understood; they didn't hate her after all.

But then her smile faded. She still had no idea what Miss Shimmery would decide. And what on earth would her parents say? They had always taught her that rules were meant to be respected.

Oh, please don't let me be expelled from Glitterwings, she thought fervently, clenching her fists. *Please!*

Chapter Nine

The next day Glitterwings Academy was abuzz with excitement. First there had been the drama of Twink and the wasp, and now their projects were due! The Great Branch was filled with items of every shape and description – beautiful paintings, petal sheets of music, cunning new inventions. The fairies ran from one to the other, exclaiming with delight.

'Oh, Bimi!' cried Twink when she saw her friend's completed project. 'It's wonderful!' The tapestry seemed alive, sparkling with images that told the history of the fairies in bright, dancing colours.

'It's really OK, isn't it?' said Bimi with a grin.

'Better than OK – it's completely glimmery!' Twink ran a finger over Queen Mab's wings, admiring the delicate stitching. 'I wish I'd had time to do a project, too,' she said wistfully. 'I'm the only fairy in the whole school who didn't.'

Bimi laughed. 'At least you didn't try to scrape something together at the last minute, like Mariella! She looks as sick as a fly now.'

Twink bit back a smile. Mariella was standing beside a hastily scribbled drawing with a sour expression on her face. Sooze high-kicked her way past her, showing off her dance. 'What's wrong, Mosquito Nose? Doesn't anyone love *your* project?'

'Oh, flap off,' snapped Mariella. 'At least I'm not going to get expelled, like *some* fairies!' She and Lola collapsed into giggles as Twink winced.

'Ignore them,' whispered Bimi.

Twink tried to smile. 'She's probably right, though, isn't she?'

'Your attention!' called Miss Shimmery from the

front of the Great Branch. 'Everyone be seated, please!'

The HeadFairy stood on a large blue mushroom that Miss Petal had grown for her. Her injured wing, though well on the mend, still looked slightly crumpled in the light of the glow-worms.

'Now then,' smiled Miss Shimmery once everyone was seated. 'I think we can all agree that the projects are an amazing success. Please give yourselves a big round of flutters!'

The fairies cheered, clapping their wings together. The flowers over each table danced in the sudden breeze, and Twink felt her breath catch. It was so beautiful here! How could she bear it if she had to leave Glitterwings for ever?

'It's been a difficult choice, but we've decided on the winners from each year,' continued Miss Shimmery. 'Mrs Lightwing, would you announce the first-year winners?'

Mrs Lightwing shot up into the air, hovering above the platform. Trying to hide her smile, she said, 'The third-place winner for the first year is . . .

Jani Sunbeam, who made a beautiful water fountain for the Common Branch! Come and get your sparkle mark, Jani.'

A small green-haired fairy from Snowdrop Branch flitted to the platform with a broad grin on her face. Mrs Lightwing handed her a shimmering silver star.

'Well done, Jani – it's both beautiful and practical. Now, fly up and add the sparkle mark to your branch's flower!'

Jani's wings hummed as she took off. Hovering beside the white snowdrop that hung over her branch's table, she flung the tiny star at it. Immediately, the star started circling about the flower, leaving a gleaming silver trail in its wake.

The Snowdrop Branch fairies cheered loudly. Their sparkle mark would shine until the end of term, letting everyone know their branch had done well.

'Second place,' said Mrs Lightwing. She paused, and looked down at the Daffodil Branch table. Twink froze as their year head's eyes met her own.

'Twink Flutterby!' announced Mrs Lightwing.

The Branch went silent. 'But – but I didn't do

anything,' stammered Twink in bewilderment.

'Come to the front, Twink,' said Miss Shimmery. Twink flew to the platform in a daze.

Miss Shimmery turned and addressed the school. 'Although Twink didn't officially do a project, we've decided that what she *did* do – taking care of the injured wasp who you all saw yesterday – was just as much for the betterment of the school. Because of her, we've seen that wasps and fairies *can* be friends – and therefore, our old hatreds need to be challenged.'

Twink felt her cheeks redden. 'But – but that's not why I did it. I just –'

Miss Shimmery smiled. 'Of course not, Twink. But you've given us all a lot to think about, and you deserve your sparkle mark.'

She motioned to Mrs Lightwing, who handed Twink a silver star. Twink gazed in wonder as the star gleamed brightly in her hand.

'Well done, girl,' said Mrs Lightwing, clapping her on the shoulder. 'And by the way, that was a nice piece of healing magic you did on the wasp's wing, too!'

'But – aren't I going to be expelled?' asked Twink. 'I broke so many rules!'

'No, Twink,' said Miss Shimmery gently. 'Rules are extremely important, but you shouldn't follow them blindly. Sometimes they have to be broken to do what's right. You followed your heart, and taught us all something as a result.'

Twink nodded slowly, taking it in.

'And I have this for you, too.' The HeadFairy handed Twink a rolled-up rose petal. 'It's a letter to you from your parents. We wrote to them by special moth-delivery last night, to tell them what happened.'

Her parents! Twink gulped as she took the letter. 'What did they say?'

A twinkle lit Miss Shimmery's eyes. 'They were as amazed as I was at how wrong one's perceptions can sometimes be.'

Twink frowned in confusion. Miss Shimmery laughed. 'They're very proud of you, my dear – as are we!'

Her parents were proud of her! A warm glow

tingled through Twink. 'There's just one thing I don't understand,' she said. 'Why was Stripe able to call to me, when wasps can't do magic?'

Miss Shimmery squeezed her shoulder. 'Friendship has a magic of its own, Twink. Stripe needed you desperately at that moment – and so you were able to hear him. Now, go and add your sparkle mark to your flower!'

Her thoughts in a whirl, Twink flitted into the air and tossed her star at the daffodil. It sped about the flower, leaving a shimmering trail behind it. The

Branch erupted into thunderous wing-clapping as Twink flew back to her seat.

Bimi hugged her tightly, bouncing on her mushroom. 'Oh, Twink! I'm so glad!'

'Imagine,' grinned Sooze, flipping back her lavender hair. 'All that sneaking about, and you get a sparkle mark for it!'

Twink glanced up at her star and laughed happily. 'I know – daft, isn't it!' She clutched the letter from her parents, eager to be alone so she could read it. But for now, it was enough to know that they were proud of her.

'Well, I think you deserve it, Opposite,' Sooze went on. 'But I bet some fairies, who shall remain *anonymous*, aren't so pleased.' Everyone laughed as Mariella and Lola scowled.

'We still have one more prize for the first year!' called Mrs Lightwing. 'The first-place winner is . . .' she paused dramatically, scanning her students, 'Bimi Bluebell, for her wonderful tapestry!'

'Oh!' Bimi started, covering her mouth with her hands.

'Go on!' said Twink, pushing her shoulder. She watched proudly as her friend flew to the platform, looking stunned and disbelieving as Mrs Lightwing handed her a shining star.

'It's a real work of art, Bimi!' said Miss Shimmery warmly. 'With your permission, we'd like to hang it in the Great Branch permanently, for all of our future students to enjoy.'

Bimi's face blazed poppy-red. 'I – yes, of course!' she gasped. 'But – but not just yet. It's not finished.'

'Not finished?' Miss Shimmery frowned. 'But it's perfect!'

Bimi shook her head. 'No, not yet. You see, I've shown the Great Wasp Wars, and – and now there's more to the story. I need to add a bit at the end, showing Twink and Stripe.'

Twink sat up straight, her pointed ears burning as she stared at Bimi. Emotion surged through her. She and Stripe, on a tapestry together for ever, for all of the Glitterwings students to see!

Miss Shimmery smiled in understanding. 'Yes, please do,' she said. 'And then we'll be proud to have it on our wall.'

The Branch cheered again as Bimi added her star to Twink's and then sat down, her face on fire.

'Thanks,' whispered Twink. She couldn't say anything else, but she knew Bimi understood. Overhead, the two stars danced together, weaving silver trails.

'Don't thank *me*,' said Bimi softly. 'You're the one who was brave enough to rescue Stripe, no matter what the rest of us said.'

Twink nodded, unable to speak. She looked at the window, missing Stripe despite herself. Where was he tonight? Flying in the moonlight with his parents, perhaps, or maybe snuggled up safely in his home.

Bimi squeezed her hand. 'He's thinking of you, too,' she whispered.

Twink smiled gratefully at her. And she knew with all her heart that it was true. No matter how old they got, or where their lives might take them . . . she and Stripe would be friends for ever.

The End

From Fairy Dust

'Isn't it great to be going back to Glitterwings?' said Twink Flutterby to her best friend, Bimi Bluebell. 'I can hardly wait to see everyone again!' Twink's lavender wings blurred as she did a quick somersault in the air.

Bimi smiled in agreement as the two fairies flew through the misty winter morning. 'We had a fabulous holiday, though, didn't we? I can't believe it's over already.'

Twink nodded, eyes shining. 'It was completely glimmery! You'll have to come to stay with us again this summer.'

Bimi had stayed with the Flutterby family for the last week of the winter holidays, and the two friends had had a wonderful time. Twink's family lived beside a stream in a grassy meadow, and she and Bimi had gone skating on the frozen water with Teena, Twink's younger sister . . .

Glitterwings Academy

Titania Woods

There are lots more stories about Glitterwings
Academy – make sure you haven't missed any of them!

If you have any difficulty in finding these in your local bookshop,
please visit www.bloomsbury.com or call 020 7440 2475
to order direct from Bloomsbury Publishing.

Visit www.glitterwingsacademy.co.uk for more fabulous fairy fun!